ZACHARY HYMAN

— Illustrated by —

ZACHARY PULLEN

# The Bambino and Me

TUNDRA BOOKS

Text copyright © 2014 by Zachary Hyman
Illustrations copyright © 2014 by Zachary Pullen

Voice-over Record: Buzzy's Recording
Sound Design Mix and Master: 6 Degrees Studios—Chris Vail
Voice Director/Producer: Christian Goutsis
Producer: Stuart Hyman, Three Lions Enterprises Inc.

Photo credit on page 46 © National Baseball Hall of Fame Library/
Major League Baseball Platinum/Getty Images
Photo frame image © Alberto Masnovo/Shutterstock

Published in Canada by Tundra Books, a division of Random House of Canada Limited,
One Toronto Street, Suite 300, Toronto, Ontario M5C 2V6

Published in the United States by Tundra Books of Northern New York,
P.O. Box 1030, Plattsburgh, New York 12901

Library of Congress Control Number: 2013940758

**Library and Archives Canada Cataloguing in Publication**

Hyman, Zachary, author
The Bambino and me / by Zachary Hyman ; illustrated by Zachary Pullen.

Issued in print and electronic formats.
ISBN 978-1-77049-627-9 (bound).—ISBN 978-1-77049-629-3 (epub)

1. Ruth, Babe, 1895-1948—Juvenile fiction.  I. Pullen, Zachary, illustrator  II. Title.

PS8615.Y527B34 2014        jC813'.6        C2013-903539-7        C2013-903540-0

Designed by Kelly Hill
The artwork in this book was rendered in oil paint and walnut oil on board.
The type was set in Filosofia.

www.tundrabooks.com

Printed and bound in China

1 2 3 4 5 6        19 18 17 16 15 14

Baseball was, is and always will be to me

the best game in the world.

—BABE RUTH, 1895–1948

I'll always remember the summer of 1927.

I was ten, and we lived in a tiny apartment above Berman's Bakery
in the Bronx. We didn't have much money, but we were a very close
family and it was a happy time.

Televisions, computers and video games hadn't been invented
yet. To pass the time, my sister practiced the piano, my brother read
adventure books and I played baseball in the park with my friends.

I loved the game, even though I wasn't very good at it and was always the last one picked for the team. I dreaded walking up to the plate 'cause I couldn't hit for beans. I was so afraid of striking out that most days I didn't even swing at the ball.

Nick the Noodle made a habit of calling me "an easy out," and whenever he did, everyone laughed at me. Sometimes I felt like giving up, but I just loved baseball too much.

The New York Yankees were the best team in professional baseball back then, and their treasure was my favorite player of all time: Babe Ruth! He was the greatest slugger who ever lived. People called him the Sultan of Swat, the King of Swing, the Great Bambino, the Babe! The crack of his bat was music to the ears of every Yankees fan.

But Babe Ruth hadn't always been a New York Yankee. Back when he was the hero of the 1916 and 1918 World Series, he played for the Boston Red Sox, the one team every Yankees fan hates to lose to. And he hadn't always been a famous slugger either. He was once the greatest pitcher in the American League, but he was moved to the outfield so he could get more turns at bat.

Every time the Babe played, he helped the Red Sox thump us. But 1919 was our lucky year. The Red Sox owner got himself into a real pickle. He needed money—and lots of it—so he sold the Babe to us. That was the best trade in the history of baseball!

Pops loved the Yankees as much as I did. We would listen to the

games on the radio together, thrilling to the whoosh of every pitch,

the crack of every bat and the thump of every foot on the bases as the

runners sprinted for home.

Pops kept promising to take me to a real game, but I knew we

didn't have the money for that. The one thing I did have was a Babe

Ruth baseball card. I won it flipping cards with Timmy Lane.

I carried the Great Bambino's card with me everywhere, never
letting it out of my sight. I always dreamt of meeting him, but I knew
that would be tougher than finding a four-leaf clover. Heck, the
Babe was more famous than Tarzan. He was every kid's hero!

On the morning of my birthday that year, I sat at the breakfast table staring into a big white bowl of bubbling, mushy porridge. *Blop, blop, blop*—it made my stomach turn. I leaned over and took a big whiff. Oh gosh, it was awful!

"George Henry Alexander, you stop smelling your food and eat up. You hear me?" snapped Ma.

When she turned her back, my brother, Freddy, dumped the rest of his own porridge into my bowl. "Yeah," he echoed. "Eat up! It's good for you!"

I was mad—real mad—so I pushed my bowl away. Underneath it was an envelope. "What's this?" I asked.

"It's from your father and me," answered Ma. "Maybe if you finish your breakfast, you'll get to open it, Babe." She used to call me Babe because I was the youngest.

That was all I needed to hear. I reached into my pocket, which was filled with all kinds of important stuff I might need—like a bunch of marbles, a couple of jacks and some bottle caps— and pulled out a clothespin. Pinching my nose shut and closing my eyes, I scooped up a blob of porridge and pretended that I was eating ice cream. I couldn't wait to open that envelope!

"Now that's better," said Ma, lifting my empty bowl off the old table. "Go ahead, then, Babe."

I ripped open the envelope. Inside I found two baseball tickets for a game between the Boston Red Sox and the New York Yankees.

My face lit up brighter than a Christmas tree!

"Happy birthday, son," Pops said with a laugh. "We're finally gonna see the Yankees play!"

I was so happy, I couldn't speak.

And my birthday wasn't over yet. Ma plunked down a big red present and said, "It's from Uncle Alvin in Boston."

Before she'd even finished her sentence I'd attacked the gift, sending scraps of paper and shreds of ribbon flying into the air like confetti.

"What's this?" I asked, holding up a gray-and-red jersey.

Ma smiled from ear to ear. "It's a baseball jersey!"

"And a bright red cap!" giggled Freddy.

Pops covered his eyes.

"It's a Boston Red Sox jersey!" I snapped.

Ma read the card aloud: "Dear George, I know how much you love baseball. Wear these well! Love, Uncle Alvin."

"I can't wear that!" I tossed the jersey back in the box as if it were Freddy's smelly underwear.

Ma gave me an earful. "You listen here, young man! Your uncle paid hard-earned money for that jersey and ball cap. You'll wear them with gratitude!"

"Baloney!" I banged the table. "I wouldn't be caught dead in those things! You may as well give them back!"

Ma was livid. "Do you want to insult Uncle Alvin? You should be ashamed of yourself!"

I stamped my feet. "It's a Red Sox jersey and a crummy cap! I can't wear a Boston Red Sox jersey!"

"It's a baseball jersey!" Ma slung the sweater across my back. "And look, it fits perfectly. If you know what's good for you, you'll wear it to the ball game tomorrow and thank Uncle Alvin for his gift. You're one lucky boy!"

"Arghhh!" My face turned beet red. "I don't wanna go to the baseball game, and I don't wanna wear this stinkin' jersey or that lousy cap. They're the worst presents ever!"

"Stinkin'? Lousy?" Ma picked up a big bar of soap and waved it about. "Don't you open your filthy mouth to me again, young man, or I'll wash it out with this here soap!"

I stood up and faced her, as mad as a wet hen. Puffing up my chest—feeling more grizzly than a grizzly bear—I screamed, "Ah, applesauce!"

That was the last time I ever talked back to my mother. I still remember the dreadful taste of that soap—Ma made sure I never forgot it!

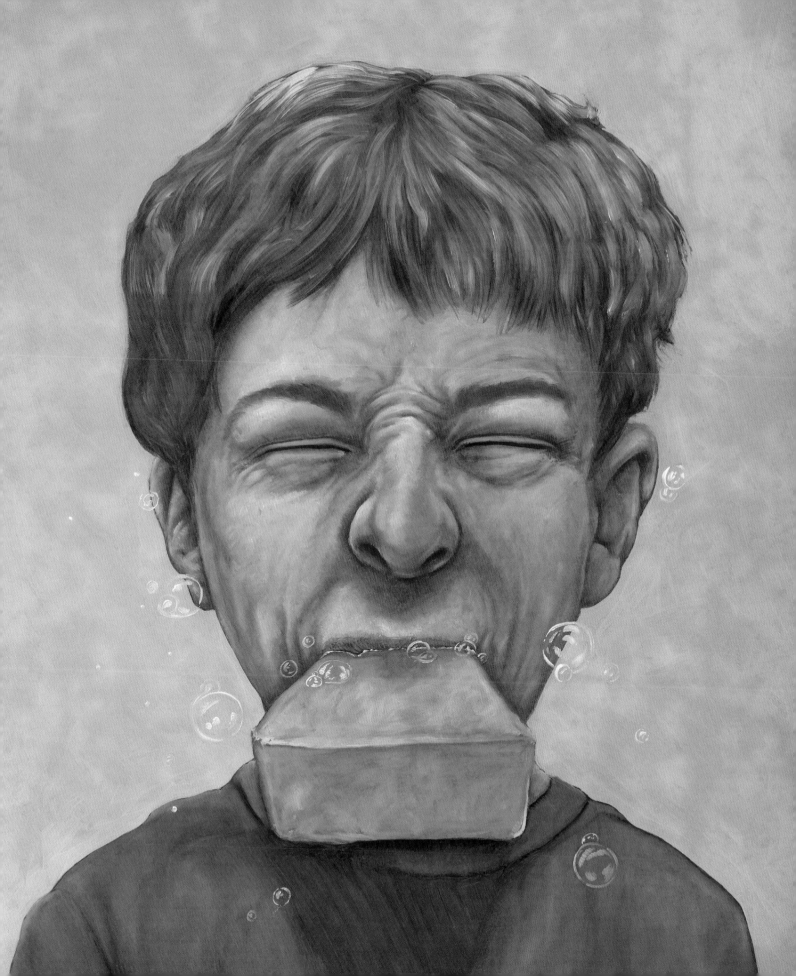

The next day should have been the greatest day ever, but in that jersey and that ball cap, I felt lower than I'd ever felt before. All those nights I'd dreamt of seeing the Babe, and now that the day was here, I wanted to be anywhere else, doing anything else.

I was about to embark on the worst journey of my young life!

The ballpark was only a few blocks away, but it felt like a hundred miles. Every step was a painful, blistering bounce. It seemed like every kid in the neighborhood was playing outside that day, and no one could miss me dressed in those DEAD SOX colors! Every diehard Yankees fan hated the Red Sox, and at that moment I was the biggest no-good, dirty rotten scoundrel in the Bronx.

Spud Bloom yelled out, "George, have you lost your mind? That's the enemy's uniform you've got on!"

"Why, you two-faced, double-crossing weasel," cried Slim Jim, shaking his fist in my direction.

Even my best pal, Murphy, looked grim. "Jeepers creepers, George!" he said. "A Red Sox jersey?"

I felt lower than an ant crawling on the pavement. I would've rather kissed a girl—*that's* how bad it was!

There were certain things a kid just didn't do, and this was one of them. Nobody dared wear a Red Sox jersey to a Yankees game. That was asking for trouble!

Once Pops and I arrived at the ballpark, my heart sank even lower. There were loads of people, all of them wearing Yankee blue and white. No one wore red except for me. I stuck out like a worm in a rotten apple.

I felt like the biggest traitor in the world. I was going to watch my hero in the colors of the team that had sold him away. Everyone was staring at me with daggers in their eyes!

Pops and I settled into our seats in the bleachers, surrounded by Yankees fans. I tried to enjoy the game, but people kept pelting me with popcorn and peanuts. Pops laughed it all off, but I couldn't. I curled down in my seat, trying to disappear.

Just then, everybody around us rose to their feet.

"I can't see! I can't see!" I hollered.

The big guy next to me hollered back, "You don't wanna see, kid. It's the Babe, and he'll wash your Sox clean!"

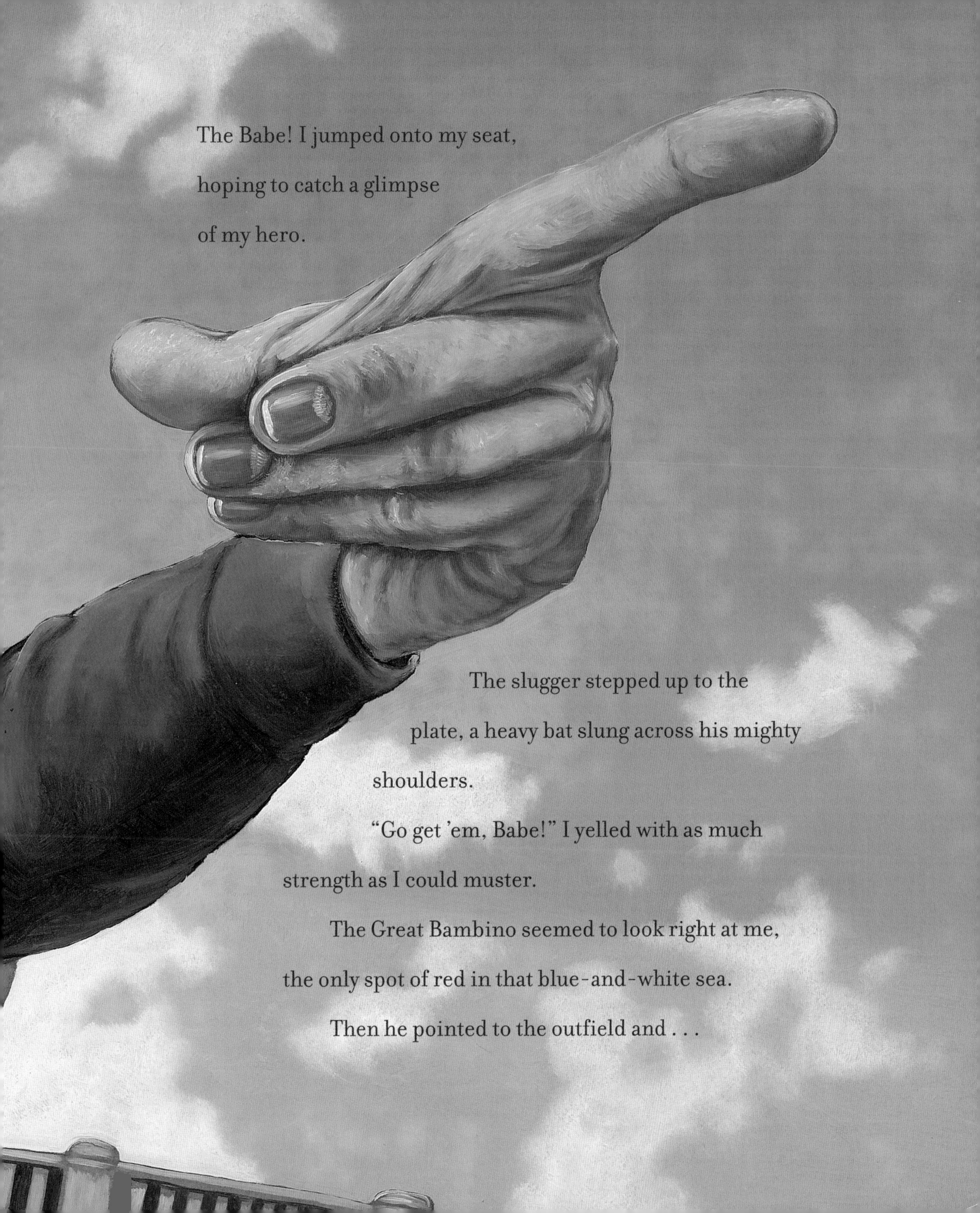

The Babe! I jumped onto my seat,

hoping to catch a glimpse

of my hero.

The slugger stepped up to the

plate, a heavy bat slung across his mighty

shoulders.

"Go get 'em, Babe!" I yelled with as much

strength as I could muster.

The Great Bambino seemed to look right at me,

the only spot of red in that blue-and-white sea.

Then he pointed to the outfield and . . .

The Babe hit the baseball so hard, it burst through the clouds! It was a towering home run, right out of the park.

The Yankees fans celebrated, and I celebrated right along with them.

"Hey, kid," shouted the big guy next to me. "You're our good luck charm!"

"Yeah," another grudgingly agreed. "You ain't so bad for a Bosox fan."

They even bought me a hot dog! I was having the most fun a kid could ever have.

And best of all, my Yankees won 10–3!

As Pops and I stood up to leave at the end of the game, some big palookas grabbed us and told us to come with them. Yikes! I knew that wearing a Red Sox uniform would get me into trouble.

After waiting in a dimly lit hallway in the depths of the stadium for what seemed like an eternity, I finally heard footsteps in the distance.

BANG! A door cracked open like a bullet, and someone stepped forward from a lighted tunnel beyond.

He was a giant, bigger than any man I had ever seen . . .

"What's your name?" came the deep, powerful voice.

I swallowed hard. "George," I squeaked.

"Mine too," said the stranger. He stepped forward into the light

and I saw his face. It was the Great Bambino himself, Babe Ruth!

"You're not really a Red Sox fan, are you, kid?" the Babe asked.

I reached into my pocket, pulling out my prized possession—my crinkled Bambino baseball card. "No sir." I shook my head forcefully. "I'm a Babe Ruth fan, sir!"

"Me too!" the Bambino said, chuckling so loudly the whole building seemed to shake. "May I?" he asked, gesturing at my card.

I handed it to him. He took out a pen, signed it and handed it back.

"Them words are magic!" he declared.

I smiled and slipped my lucky card back into my pocket.

The Babe put his hand on my shoulder. "So what d'ya wanna be when you grow up, son?"

"A slugger just like you, Babe!" I said. Then I lowered my head. "But I ain't any good. I always strike out."

"Well, in that case, you'll need this." The Babe lifted his cap and put it on my head. Then he took off his famous Yankees jersey and draped it around my shoulders.

Then the Great Bambino leaned down and whispered, "Listen, kid. Don't let the fear of striking out hold you back. I swing big, with everything I've got. I hit big or I miss big. Every strike brings me closer to the next home run." He straightened back up and gave me a wink. "If you try hard enough, you're bound to come out on top!"

Many years have passed, but I still carry that Babe Ruth card, tucked neatly away in my wallet. Whenever I feel blue, I reach in, pull out my lucky card and think about those magic words:

"It's hard to beat a person who never gives up!"

Many people still think George Herman "Babe" Ruth was the greatest baseball player who ever lived. He played in the major leagues for twenty-two seasons, setting numerous records along the way. In that magical 1927 season, the year this story is set, he hit sixty home runs, a record that stood for more than thirty years.

Although the meeting between George and the Great Bambino is imagined, I have used many of the famous man's own words to tell it. Babe Ruth loved kids as much as he loved baseball, and he never hesitated to give them advice on how to succeed in life, just as he does George in the story.

Babe Ruth continues to inspire the young and the old to this day, compelling us to keep swinging big with everything we've got so we can hit our home runs and make our dreams come true. The Babe inspired me too, and that's why I wrote this book. I never saw him play, never heard the crack of his bat, but his words of wisdom echo in my head and in my heart. And as I wrote these pages, I couldn't help thinking there was a towering giant leaning over my shoulder and whispering in my ear, telling me to keep swinging till I hit a home run.

—ZACHARY HYMAN

*Heroes are remembered*

*but legends never die.*

—BABE RUTH